To my grandmother, Dorothy Holabird KH
To my grandsons, Nat and Will, with love HC

Published by Pleasant Company Publications
© 2000 HIT Entertainment PLC
Text copyright © 1985 Katharine Holabird
Illustrations copyright © 1985 Helen Craig

Visit our Web sites at **americangirl.com** and **angelinaballerina.com**

Printed in Italy.
01 02 03 04 05 06 07 LEGO 10 9 8 7 6 5 4 3

Library of Congress Cataloging-in-Publication Data
Craig, Helen.
Angelina's Christmas / illustrations by Helen Craig ;
story by Katharine Holabird.
p. cm.
Summary: Angelina and her cousin Henry help
bring Christmas to a lonely old postman.
ISBN 1-58485-140-6
[1. Christmas—Fiction. 2. Letter carriers—Fiction.
3. Cousins—Fiction. 4. Mice—Fiction.]
I. Holabird, Katharine. II. Title.
PZ7.C84418 Ar 2000
[E]—dc21   00-022878

Angelina's Christmas

Story by Katharine Holabird   Illustrations by Helen Craig

PLEASANT
COMPANY
PUBLICATIONS™

Christmas was coming, and everyone at Angelina's school was working hard to prepare for the Christmas show. Angelina and the other children stayed after their lessons to rehearse and help decorate the hall.

When Angelina left school it was already dark outside. Large snowflakes were falling and Angelina was so excited that she danced along the pavement.

The cottages in the village looked warm and welcoming, with holly wreaths on the doors and Christmas lights shining in all the windows; but the very last cottage was cold and dark. Angelina peeped in the window and saw an old man huddled by a tiny fire.

Angelina ran the rest of the way home and found her mother and little cousin Henry in the kitchen. She asked her mother about the man who lived all alone in the cottage.

"Oh, that's Mr. Bell," her mother replied. "He used to be the village postman, but he's too old to work now."

Angelina decided that she wanted to make a Christmas surprise for Mr. Bell, so Mrs. Mouseling gave her some dough to make biscuits shaped like stars, bells, and trees.

Henry had a piece of dough too, and he made a nice big Father Christmas biscuit. "Look!" he said proudly. "I'm going to see Father Christmas tonight and give him this biscuit *myself!*"

"Father Christmas only comes very late at night after everyone has gone to bed," Angelina explained. "Why don't you leave your special biscuit out on a plate for him?"

Henry started to cry. "No!" he shouted. "I want to see Father Christmas!"

"Don't be such a crybaby, Henry," Angelina scolded, but Henry wouldn't stop crying.

Next afternoon Angelina and her mother packed a
basket with the biscuits, mince pies, and fruit for
Mr. Bell. "Don't you want to help Angelina take the
presents to Mr. Bell?" asked Mrs. Mouseling, but
Henry only shook his head.

Then Angelina and her father went out to find a
Christmas tree for Mr. Bell. Henry followed Angelina
and Mr. Mouseling all the way to Mr. Bell's cottage,
but he still wouldn't speak to them.

The old postman was amazed and delighted to see his visitors. He invited Angelina and her father inside, and then he noticed Henry standing alone in the snow. "Come in, my friend!" said Mr. Bell with a smile, and he picked Henry up and brought him in near the fire.

Mr. Bell's eyes were bright and twinkling. "Wait here a moment," he said, and disappeared up the stairs. Then he came down looking…

…just like FATHER CHRISTMAS!

"This is the red costume I wore once when Father Christmas needed someone to take his place at the village Christmas party," said Mr. Bell with a chuckle, and he sat down with Henry on his knee. While Mr. Mouseling made tea and Angelina decorated the tree, Henry listened to Mr. Bell's stories.

"I used to go out on my bicycle, no matter what the weather was like, to deliver presents to all the children in the countryside. One year there was a terrible snowstorm and all the roads were covered with snow. I had to deliver the toys on a sled, and if I hadn't glimpsed the village lights blinking in the distance, I would have been lost out in the storm." Henry listened with wide eyes.

When it was time to go, Henry reached into his pocket. "I made this," he said, "and I'd like to give it to you." Out of his pocket he took his big Father Christmas biscuit and gave it to Mr. Bell.

"This is the best Christmas surprise I've had for many years," said Mr. Bell, thanking Henry and Angelina for their presents. Angelina said she wished Mr. Bell would come to her school show in his Father Christmas costume.

"That would be a pleasure," he said, smiling.

Mr. Bell kept his promise. He came to the Christmas
show in his red costume and watched Angelina and her

friends dressed as sugar plum fairies dancing the
Nutcracker Suite.

Later all the children gathered round Mr. Bell, and
Henry felt proud as Mr. Bell handed out the Christmas
presents and entertained everyone with stories about
his adventures as a postman.

Mr. Bell was never lonely at Christmas again, because every year he was invited to come to Angelina's school show dressed as Father Christmas.